I'm Going To READ!™

These levels are meant only as guides;
you and your child can best choose a book that's right.

Level 1: Kindergarten–Grade 1 . . . Ages 4–6
- word bank to highlight new words
- consistent placement of text to promote readability
- easy words and phrases
- simple sentences build to make simple stories
- art and design help new readers decode text

Level 2: Grade 1 . . . Ages 6–7
- word bank to highlight new words
- rhyming texts introduced
- more difficult words, but vocabulary is still limited
- longer sentences and longer stories
- designed for easy readability

Level 3: Grade 2 . . . Ages 7–8
- richer vocabulary of up to 200 different words
- varied sentence structure
- high-interest stories with longer plots
- designed to promote independent reading

Level 4: Grades 3 and up . . . Ages 8 and up
- richer vocabulary of more than 300 different words
- short chapters, multiple stories, or poems
- more complex plots for the newly independent reader
- emphasis on reading for meaning

LEVEL 3

Library of Congress Cataloging-in-Publication Data Available

2 4 6 8 10 9 7 5 3 1

Published by Sterling Publishing Co., Inc.
387 Park Avenue South, New York, NY 10016
Text copyright © 2006 by Harriet Ziefert Inc.
Illustrations copyright © 2006 by Andrea Baruffi
Article by Mark Kreigel, copyright © 1988, NY Daily News, Inc.
Reprinted with permission.
Distributed in Canada by Sterling Publishing
c/o Canadian Manda Group, 165 Dufferin Street
Toronto, Ontario, Canada M6K 3H6
Distributed in Great Britain and Europe by Chris Lloyd at Orca Book
Services, Stanley House, Fleets Lane, Poole BH15 3AJ, England
Distributed in Australia by Capricorn Link (Australia) Pty. Ltd.
P.O. Box 704, Windsor, NSW 2756, Australia

I'm Going To Read is a trademark of Sterling Publishing Co., Inc.

Sterling ISBN 13: 978-1-4027-2107-6
Sterling ISBN 10: 1-4027-2107-2

For information about custom editions, special sales, premium and
corporate purchases, please contact Sterling Special Sales
Department at 800-805-5489 or specialsales@sterlingpub.com.

Henry's Wrong Turn

Pictures by Andrea Baruffi

Sterling Publishing Co., Inc.

New York

This is Henry, a big humpback whale.
One day he made a wrong turn.

Instead of going
out to sea, he went up
the Hudson River
and right into
New York Harbor.

No one knew why Henry
wanted to be in New York Harbor.
It was busy. Very busy.
And there wasn't much
for him to eat.

A tugboat captain noticed Henry
swimming toward a bridge.

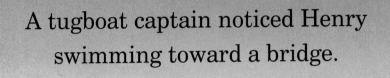

He signaled to the other boats:
Watch out for the whale!

Then Henry swam toward
the Statue of Liberty.

"Look! Look! A whale!"
shouted one of the visitors.

Henry cut in front of a big ocean liner.
The big boat's captain sounded a horn,
and Henry dove under the water.

Someone radioed the
Coast Guard for help.

The Coast Guard sent
a boat to follow Henry.

Henry swam away from the cutter
and away from a big aircraft carrier.

Everyone watched as Henry
spouted water from his blowhole.
Maybe he was trying to say,
You can't catch me!

Where's Henry now?

He's gone.
He's disappeared!

But not for long!

Henry swam downtown,
where there was lots of boat traffic.
Henry was not in a safe place.

"Watch out,
Henry!"

"Watch out for the ferries!"

"Turn around, Henry.
Or you could be struck
by a propeller!"

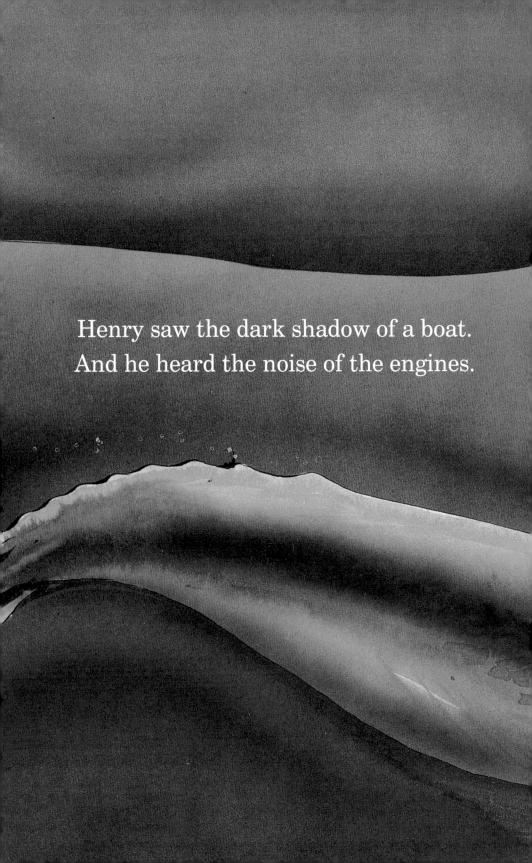

Henry saw the dark shadow of a boat.
And he heard the noise of the engines.

Do you know what he did?
He turned around!

Henry swam fast—
faster than the boats
that were on his tail.

As he left the harbor,
he dove under the water.

Good-bye,

Henry.